SUPERTATO

VEGGIES ASSEMBLE

For Max

SIMON & SCHUSTER
First published in Great Britain in 2016
by Simon & Schuster UK Ltd
1st Floor, 222 Gray's Inn Road, London, WC1X 8HB
A CBS Company

A CIP catalogue record for this book is available
from the British Library upon request

978-1-4711-2100-5 (PB)
978-1-4711-2102-9 (eBook)

Printed in Italy

9 10

SUPERTATO
VEGGIES ASSEMBLE

by Sue Hendra and Paul Linnet

SIMON & SCHUSTER

London New York Sydney Toronto New Delhi

It was night-time in the supermarket and everyone was sleeping peacefully . . . or were they?

Someone was looking for trouble.
"*Mwah ha ha ha ha*, soon this supermarket will be mine, **ALL** mine!"

And with one **click**,
ALL the freezers were switched off.

GASP!

FREEZERS

ON

OFF

You may already know this, but some vegetables are frozen for a very good reason. If they defrost they turn bad – really bad.

And baddest of them all is The Evil Pea!

"Wakey wakey!" he called.

One evil pea is bad enough.

But now there were BAGS of them!

The supermarket was in meltdown.

"Run for it!" panicked Pepper.

"S . . . S . . . SAVE ME!"
stuttered Pear.

"SAVE ME!"
begged Melon.

"SAVE ME!"
cried Carrot.

"I'M MELTING!"
pleaded Lolly.
"And time's running out!"

Was there anyone
who could save them?

But, before Supertato could save anyone,
he was attacked by a swarm of peas!

"What's going on?" asked Aubergine.
"We're DOOMED, that's what!" cried Cucumber.

Things were going from bad to worse.

Supertato was thrown on to the conveyor belt . . .

. . . and he was heading straight for the bagging area!

Was this the end for Supertato?

"I'm going . . .

to need . . .

some . . .

backup.

   If I can just . . .

      call the . . ."

CLICK!

SUPERVEGGIES
TO THE RESCUE

They used ninja know-how!

HI-YA!

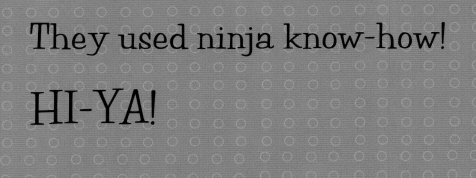

They used
MASSIVE
muscles!

Hrrr!

They used
fancy footwork.

And they used a box
with a door cut in it.

PEA PARTY

But what about the lollies? And where was Supertato?

"Sorry I'm late, I just needed to pick up some dessert!"

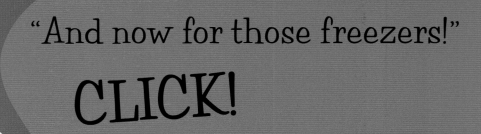

"And now for those freezers!"

CLICK!

"And I'll be needing a glass and a piece of paper." Eh?

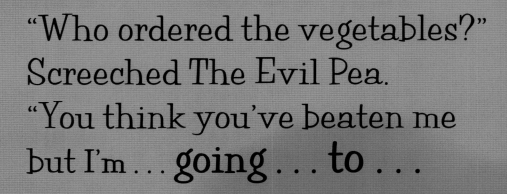

"Who ordered the vegetables?" Screeched The Evil Pea. "You think you've beaten me but I'm . . . going . . . to . . .

. . . Hmmmmmmmmppfff!"

"You're going to do what?" asked Supertato.

"Three cheers for Supertato!" shouted Broccoli.
Supertato blushed. "I couldn't have done it without
the Superveggies."

"Actually, I'm not a vegetable, I'm a fruit," said Tomato.
And everybody laughed and cheered.

So, with the peas back in their bags
and the freezers locked . . .

. . . the supermarket was once again a safe place to be.

"Isn't it wonderful," said one lolly to the other.
"We're all back to normal again!"